WELCOME TO

Beast Quest

Collect the special coins in this book.
You will earn one gold coin for
every chapter you read.

Once you have finished all the chapters,
find out what to do with your gold coins at
the back of the book.

With special thanks to Conrad Mason

For Beir Heathcote

www.beastquest.co.uk

ORCHARD BOOKS

First published in Great Britain in 2017 by The Watts Publishing Group

1 3 5 7 9 10 8 6 4 2

Text © 2017 Beast Quest Limited.
Cover and inside illustrations by Steve Sims
© Beast Quest Limited 2017

Beast Quest is a registered trademark of Beast Quest Limited
Series created by Beast Quest Limited, London

A CIP catalogue record for this book is available from the British Library.

ISBN 978 1 40834 317 3

Printed and bound by CPI Group (UK) Ltd, Croydon, CR0 4YY

The paper and board used in this book are made from wood from responsible sources.

Orchard Books
An imprint of Hachette Children's Group
Part of The Watts Publishing Group Limited
Carmelite House, 50 Victoria Embankment, London EC4Y 0DZ

An Hachette UK Company
www.hachette.co.uk
www.hachettechildrens.co.uk

STRYTOR
THE SKELETON
DRAGON

BY ADAM BLADE

ORCHARD

JUNGLE OF FEAR

TUNNEL OF DOUBT

ICY CLIFFS

FROZEN OCEAN

CONTENTS

When I was a young apprentice wizard, there was a secret chamber my master forbade me to enter. But even then, I did not like being told what to do. With a simple unlocking spell, I found my way in.

I was very disappointed. For that room contained no potions or poisons, no magical weapons. All I saw was a single oval stone, grey and speckled, lying on a cushion.

My master found me. To my surprise, he did not beat or curse me. Instead he smiled.

"Jezrin," he said, "behold the key to immeasurable power!"

"What, an old rock?" I replied.

At that, his face turned grave. "That is no rock, apprentice. That is a dragon egg. And one day it will allow you to spread Evil to every corner of every kingdom."

As he led me from the room, I was not impressed. My master never lived to see the egg hatch. But his promise proved true.

The time of Evil has come. And nothing – no one – can stand in my path.

BETRAYAL IN THE NIGHT

"I've never seen you so pale," said Elenna, peering anxiously at Tom. "Are you all right?"

Tom's right hand pulsed with pain, but he nodded and rose from the boulder where he'd been resting.

"He always has to be such a hero, doesn't he?" muttered Petra, sarcastically.

Elenna shot a warning look at the young witch, but Petra ignored it. Her blood-red crow, Rourke, ruffled his feathers and squawked harshly from her shoulder.

"I'm fine, really," said Tom, through gritted teeth. "Let's keep going."

An orange sun shone low in the sky as they set out again, journeying along the bottom of a steep, rocky valley. Just that morning they had left behind the darkness of the jungle, where Tom had battled Vetrix. He had defeated the Beast, but in return the poison dragon had given him a savage bite on the wrist of his sword arm.

Tom shivered and rolled up his sleeve. His whole arm was swollen with venom, and hard brown scales stretched from wrist to elbow. The wound throbbed, and the blood in Tom's veins was as cold as ice water.

But we can't stop now. Their enemy Jezrin was getting closer and closer to the Well of Power. If the Evil Wizard drank from it, they would stand no chance of stopping him. *First he'll take control of Drakonia, then Avantia, and then...*

Tom flinched as another wave of pain swept through his body.

"That does it," said Elenna, stopping suddenly. "We're not going any further until you're better."

"Agreed," said Petra. "You look awful. And that wound is really starting to stink."

"I told you, I can go on," Tom protested, but he couldn't help shuddering. "Besides, if Jezrin gets too far ahead—"

"Never mind Jezrin," Petra
interrupted. "He might be evil, but
he's also old. He'll need to rest too.
Anyway – legend says, the Well of
Power is guarded by an invincible
dragon. Jezrin wouldn't dare go
charging in without a plan."

Rourke cawed from Petra's
shoulder, as though in agreement.

"They're right, Tom," said Elenna.
"We need you fighting fit if we're
going to stop Jezrin. Come on,
Master of the Beasts. Let's get you
lying down."

Tom wanted to argue, but he
didn't have the strength. Elenna laid
out a blanket and bunched up her

travelling pack as a pillow. Then she helped Tom down on to the makeshift bed, where he lay clutching his injured arm.

"It'll be dark soon," said Elenna, wrapping the blanket around him. "I'll find some wood and make a fire."

"Who needs wood?" scoffed Petra.

"I'll take care of this."

The witch flung out her hand, and the boulder next to Tom burst into bright purple flames. Her crow took flight in surprise, perching on the rocky ground nearby.

Elenna and Petra crouched beside Tom, their faces lit purple. "I'll be

better in no time," Tom told them.
"Just a little break, then we'll head
off again…" But he felt his muscles
relax in the warm glow of the fire,
and his head sank on to Elenna's
pack. He looked up at the sky, which
was turning deep blue in the twilight.
Gradually the pain ebbed away, and
Tom's eyes began to close.

As he drifted off, he heard Petra
murmuring in a low voice. "I think
he's asleep now."

"Is he going to make it?" asked
Elenna.

"I've no idea," Petra replied. "That
arm doesn't look very healthy, does
it?"

Tom tried to tell them he was all

right, but he couldn't seem to make his lips move.

At last, he fell into a deep sleep.

"Hey! Come back here!"

Tom woke, pushing himself upright. Pain stabbed through his hand, and he gasped out loud.

The sky was black and starless, but purple flames still flickered from the boulder. In the eerie half-light, Tom saw the dark figure of Petra rush past, waving her arms wildly. "I won't tell you again!" she yelled.

"He's getting away," shouted Elenna. Tom turned to see his friend fitting an arrow to her bow.

"Don't you dare!" roared Petra. The witch thrust out both hands, and a powerful gust of wind whirled from her fingers, making Elenna stumble. Her bowstring hummed, and the arrow skittered off course.

Tom rose unsteadily. "What's going on?" he demanded.

"It's that horrible crow," said Elenna. "He's flying off with everything – Quarg's horn, Vetrix's scale and Korvax's ice fang!"

Tom felt a cold tingle creep up his spine. *The magical tokens!* He scanned the night sky and spotted the distant shape of Rourke, flapping off into the darkness, with a loaded sack dangling from his talons. "Can't

you call him back?" he asked Petra.

"What do you think I'm trying to do?" snapped the witch. "He won't listen to me!"

"This was your plan all along,

wasn't it?" Elenna shouted. "You wanted to steal the magical tokens for yourself!"

"Nonsense," said Petra. "I don't know what's got into him!"

"But I do," said a deep, familiar voice.

Tom, Elenna and Petra all whirled around.

That was Jezrin's voice, thought Tom. But the old wizard was nowhere to be seen.

"That's a nasty wound," sneered the voice. Tom saw that Rourke had circled in the air and was now hovering in the sky above them, still grasping the sack with his talons.

The Evil Wizard must be talking

through the crow!

Rourke opened his beak and spoke again. "Funny how much trouble a little nip can cause."

"He's taken control of my pet," whispered Petra. Her lips trembled with anger.

"Rourke was always mine, foolish girl!" said the crow, in Jezrin's voice. "And so are these prizes from the three dragons you faced! I should really thank you for fighting so hard for them. And now, if you'll excuse me, it is time for me to make the final journey to the Well of Power. But don't worry, friends, I won't forget you... You shall be the very first to die!"

CHASING THE CROW

"What are we waiting for?" snapped Petra. "We can't let Jezrin steal my crow!"

"Not to mention the magical tokens," said Elenna. "That bird must have been working for Jezrin from the start. He used Rourke to lure us here to Drakonia."

Tom was struck by a terrible thought. "Jezrin said he was going to the Well of Power," he said. "You don't think those tokens will give him the magic he needs to raise it?"

Elenna went pale. "I don't know, but I'd rather not find out. Petra's right – let's get after that bird!"

Grabbing their packs, they set off into the darkness, heading in the direction that Rourke had flown. In the distance, Tom could see shadowy mountain peaks rising at the end of the valley. The thought of the climb brought pain rushing back into his hand, but he ignored it, along with the icy cold running through his veins. With the Quest ahead of them, he was feeling a little stronger. *We've got to stop Jezrin before he reaches the well!*

The sky grew lighter as they journeyed through the valley, and at last they began to climb, following a rugged pathway which wound up a mountainside. Tom's hand was throbbing more with every step, but there was no way he was going to stop now.

The first rays of dawn peeked out above the mountain, turning the rocks pink. It was beautiful, but Tom couldn't enjoy it.

Something's not right...

The thought came from nowhere and stopped him dead in his tracks.

"What's wrong?" said Elenna, looking at him anxiously. "Is it your hand?"

Tom glanced round. The path had become much narrower. To their right the rock face rose steeply upwards. To their left, it fell away in a sheer cliff. There was no sign of danger.

But still...

"Do you feel like we're being watched?" asked Tom.

"You're imagining things," said Petra. "There's no one here but us."

The witch was right. Some vultures circled in the sky, but apart from that they were alone.

"Sorry," said Tom. "Let's just keep on going."

He took a step forward, then froze. Two large, muscular figures had appeared on the path ahead. For a moment Tom thought they were made out of rock, until he recognised the tough, lizard-like scales of the Drakonians.

They must have been lying in

wait for us, camouflaged against the mountainside!

"Nobody move," growled the bigger of the two Drakonians, his tongue flickering between sharp, yellow teeth. "This is our mountain!" He had plates of spiked bone lashed to his forearms like claws. His companion held a thickly knotted net made out of vines.

"Let us pass," said Elenna. "We don't want a fight."

"Then you'd better surrender!" snarled a voice from behind.

Tom whirled round and saw two more Drakonians blocking the pathway behind, both armed with heavy wooden clubs.

"I'll handle them," said Elenna, fitting an arrow to her bowstring. "You take the others!"

The big Drakonian lunged forwards, slicing with a bone claw. Tom drew his sword and swung it with his brown-scaled fist, but the Drakonian easily swept Tom's blade aside. The sword struck a rock and juddered, sending a stab of agony through Tom's poisoned hand.

The Drakonian slammed his full weight into Tom, shoving him against the mountainside. Then he pushed a bone claw up against Tom's neck, so hard that he could barely breathe.

Tom struggled, but he was so much weaker than normal. He could only

watch, helpless, as the Drakonian
with the net tossed it over Petra.
The witch had raised her hands to
cast a spell, but the net knocked her
to the ground before she could use
her magic.

Elenna loosed her arrow, but it

glanced off a rock and flew out over the mountainside. One of her attackers swung his club, knocking the bow from her hands. The other stepped behind Elenna and threw his arm around her, lifting her, kicking, into the air. "Get off me!"

growled Elenna, but the Drakonian held on tight.

Tom threw all his strength into one mighty push with his left arm. Caught off guard, the big Drakonian stumbled backwards. Tom unhooked his shield and flailed with his sword, but the Drakonian parried the clumsy blow with a bone claw.

Before Tom could strike again, the other claw slammed hard into his shield, and he staggered away, reeling. The Drakonian was much stronger than he was. The lizard man swiped again and again, driving Tom back to the very brink of the precipice.

Got to...fight back!

But the Drakonian swung his spiked tail round, fast and low. It smacked into Tom's legs, knocking him off balance.

"No!" yelled Elenna and Petra, at

the same time.

Tom's heart raced as he tipped over the edge, then fell, plummeting from the pathway.

This is it... He closed his eyes, bracing for the deadly impact as he felt his body dropping, faster and faster.

THUMP!

He landed suddenly on his back. Pain exploded through him. For a few moments he lay dazed, unable to move, staring at the sky. Every bone in his body ached, but he was alive. He could hardly believe it.

I must have hit a ledge on the way down!

As he caught his breath, Tom heard

the voices of the Drakonians on the pathway above. "Is the boy dead?" growled one.

The big Drakonian laughed. "That soft little worm? Not even a lizard man could survive a fall like that."

"Let's kill the others," said a third.

Tom strained his muscles to stand, but he felt dizzy with the effort and collapsed back again.

"Not yet," said the Drakonian leader. "They are our prisoners now. They will feed the skeleton dragon."

"You are too cruel, Eshra," said the first Drakonian.

Tom held his breath, listening as hard as he could. *Skeleton dragon... I don't like the sound of that.*

"If we do not spare them now," said the leader, "Strytor will be hungry. Do you wish to feed him yourself, Chakta?"

The first lizard-man said nothing.

"As I thought," said the leader. "This way our tribe will be safe. Come, we will take the Avantians to their doom."

Tom let his breath out slowly, lying still as the Drakonians dragged his friends away up the mountainside. When he could hear nothing more, he made a silent promise to himself.

While there's blood in my veins, I'll rescue them both...or I'll die trying!

VALLEY OF BONES

The sun climbed higher in the sky as
Tom lay recovering.

Got to get my strength back.

It seemed like an eternity until
most of the pain had ebbed away,
but at last, slowly, he pushed himself
upright. His back felt as though it
was on fire. His arms still ached from
the fight with the Drakonian and his

hand pulsed with Vetrix's poison. But none of that mattered.

Elenna and Petra are in trouble, and it's up to me to get them out of it.

Tom rose on weak legs and hobbled across the narrow ledge, taking care not to glance down at the dizzying drop below. Searching the cliff face, he found gaps big enough for his fingers and began to haul himself upwards. He climbed carefully, forcing himself not to rush. *If I fall now, it really will be the end...*

At last he heaved himself back up on to the mountain path. The Drakonians were nowhere to be seen. No time to rest. Tom scoured the ground until he found dusty tracks leading up the mountainside.

Using his sword as a walking stick, Tom followed the footprints of the Drakonians. The sun beat down, and he began to sweat as mid-morning drew on. He climbed higher and higher, his legs aching, until at last the tracks led him to the top of a rise. Beyond, a rocky plateau stretched out into the far distance, surrounded by mountains.

Tom drew in a sharp breath. The plateau was covered with bones. Some were ancient and yellowed. Others were fresh and white, with flesh still clinging to them. Here and there Tom saw that the bones had been crushed, as though by the feet

of some giant creature. He saw the
shattered skeletons of sheep, horses,
and... *Is that a human skull?*

A chill crept up his spine. *This
must be the hunting ground of a
dragon-Beast.*

Tom drew on the magic of the golden helmet, scanning the plateau with vision many times more powerful than his normal eyesight. *There!* Elenna and Petra were lying among the bones, their wrists and ankles bound with thick rope. The lizard-men must have already left the plateau.

Tom began to stumble across the rocks, the bones crunching beneath his boots. *I have to get to my friends before Strytor does!* Drawing on the power of the golden leg armour, he ran with magical speed, covering the distance within seconds.

"Tom!" gasped Elenna. "We thought you were dead! How did you—"

"Never mind that," Petra interrupted. "You're here now, so hurry up and untie us!"

Tom got to work, sawing through the ropes with his sword blade. Soon Elenna and Petra were scrambling to their feet, rubbing at their wrists.

I sssee you, Massster of the Beastsss...

Tom froze. The hissing voice seemed to have come from inside his head. "Did you hear that?" he asked. He turned round, but no one was there.

The sky seemed to have darkened, and a chill hung in the air.

"Are you imagining things again?" asked Petra. "We should really take a look at that hand of yours."

Tom frowned. *It's the voice of Strytor. I'm sure of it!* The Beast had to be somewhere close by. But he couldn't see him – and there was nowhere he could be hiding on the vast, empty plateau. "I heard a voice through the red jewel," he explained.

"The Drakonians said something about a dragon," said Elenna. "But where is he?"

The voice spoke again. *I'm coming, Massster... I'll pick your bonesss clean...*

"Wait," said Tom. A nasty thought had struck him. "He's called Strytor the Skeleton Dragon, isn't he?"

"So what?" said Petra, with an edge

of fear in her voice.

"So I think I know where he might be hiding," murmured Tom. "Quickly, both of you, get ready to—"

He was interrupted by a rattling of bones. Whirling round, Tom saw a mound of skeletons stirring, several horse-lengths away from them. Something was rising up from beneath, knocking the bones aside until it emerged and hovered in mid-air, level with Tom's face.

Tom heard Elenna gasp, and Petra mutter to herself in horror. He stood firm, rooted to the spot.

They were face to face with an enormous skull, yellowed with age, with savage spiked teeth and long curving horns. Its eye sockets were dark, gaping caverns, and Tom could sense malevolence burning deep inside them.

Somehow he knew immediately

what it was. *The skull of Strytor...*

SNAP! The Beast's jaw hinged
and swung shut. Then Tom watched
in horror as more bones scraped
and slid across the plateau, rising,
hovering in the air behind the skull.

First came a spine, *click-clack*ing
into place, one bone at a time. It
swayed like a snake, the tail curving
into the sky. Then more bones rose up
to form a colossal ribcage and sturdy
legs, ending in sharpened claws.
Finally, gigantic wings took shape,
slender bones hooked like fingers,
beating the air with a sound like a
thousand whips cracking.

At last the terrible clattering
sounds echoed into silence, and the

fourth and final Beast of Drakonia stood before them – the horrifying skeleton of a dragon, glowing white against the darkened sky.

It isss a long time sssince I've tasssted Avantian flessshhh... said the voice in Tom's head. *Behold your doom, Massster of the Beastsss!*

1

THE SKELETON DRAGON

"How are we supposed to defeat a skeleton?" muttered Petra.

Tom tried to flex the fingers around his sword hilt. *No good...* His hand was becoming even more stiff and numb from Vetrix's poison. *But I've got to fight Strytor!*

Quickly he shifted the sword to

his good left hand and took his shield in his right. Then he stepped in front of his companions, raising his blade.

Strytor stalked forward, bones scraping together as he moved. His tail came flicking round, surging towards Tom's head. Tom dived, crunching face-first into the bones

that lay scattered on the ground. The tail whistled as it curved overhead.

That was too close! Tom breathed in deep and almost gagged at the stench of death coming from the bones beneath him.

"Look out!" cried Elenna.

Tom glanced up and saw that a glimmer of fire had ignited deep in the hollow of the dragon's ribcage. The flames swirled, grew into a raging ball, then surged up through Strytor's neck. Tom braced himself, ready for the fire to come roaring from the Beast's mouth and engulf him...

But instead, Petra stepped in front of Tom, flinging her hands out at the

Beast. An icy blue light arced from her fingertips and struck the flames emerging from Strytor's mouth with a deafening hiss, like a blacksmith plunging a red-hot sword into a butt of water.

Strytor jerked his head back as the flame fizzled out. The Beast opened his jaws wide and let out an unearthly howl of fury, making bones rattle all across the plain. Before Petra could duck, Strytor struck her with his wing, tossing her aside like a rag doll.

Elenna loosed an arrow, but it just bounced off Strytor's shoulder blade. The skeleton dragon kicked out with a massive claw, scooping up bones from the ground and flinging them at her. Elenna dropped her bow and threw up her arms, as the rain of missiles sent her staggering backwards.

Seizing his chance, Tom jumped up

and ran behind the skeleton dragon, heading for his tail. He held out both arms for balance, then leapt on to the tail and ran unsteadily along the Beast's spine, until he reached Strytor's skull.

It's now or never... He brought his sword flashing down, as hard as he could.

THUNK! Tom's sword bounced off the skull, juddering in his hand. Strytor bucked hard, and Tom lost his footing. He tumbled from the skeleton dragon's back, smacking into a cluster of skeletons next to Petra. Strytor shrieked in fury and took off, flapping his wings frantically as though he didn't understand what had happened.

Petra was just rising groggily to her feet. "What now?" she asked, wincing and clutching at her ribs.

Tom had no answer. *Even if I could use my right hand properly, Strytor would still be too strong for us! It's as though he doesn't have a weakness. Unless...*

As the dragon circled in the air, Tom peered at the joints between his bones and saw flashes of red connecting them together. *If I could cut some of those tendons, maybe Strytor might collapse!*

But to do that, he would have to somehow get up close to the Beast without being scorched by his breath...

Elenna had picked up her bow and was notching another arrow as the skeleton dragon swooped down to land again. Tom cupped his hands and called out to her. "Stay clear! I've got a plan."

"I just hope it's a good one!" Elenna shouted back. She ducked down, taking cover behind a heap of blackened bones.

Me too, thought Tom. "Petra, can you create a diversion?"

The witch nodded grimly, then flung out her hands and sent another magical bolt of blue light searing towards Strytor.

As the skeleton dragon hissed and recoiled, Tom called on the power of

the golden leg armour. He sprinted
with magical speed, until he was
right underneath Strytor's ribcage.
Looking up, he saw a mass of the
red tendons connecting each rib to
the Beast's breastbone. *It's going
to take all the strength I've got to
break them...*

Tom crouched, then leapt as high
as he could. At the same instant
he clenched his poisoned fist tight,
ignoring the pain as he drew on the
power of his golden breastplate.
With a burst of magical strength,
he drove his fist into the breastbone
like a battering ram.

CRACK!

Tom felt the breastbone fracture

as it was forced upwards. The
tendons all tore in one go, and the
dragon let out another terrible howl
of fury as his ribs swung free.

Dropping to the ground, Tom rolled aside. The earth shook beneath him as Strytor crumbled, until at last the thunder of falling bones gave way to silence.

Tom lay, panting, feeling utterly drained. Looking back, he saw the jumbled heap of bones which had been Strytor only moments before. Deep within, the last of the fire flickered, as a hissing voice spoke weakly in Tom's head. *He mussst not reach the well...*

Then it trailed off into nothing, and the last glimmer of fire burned out.

"You did it! You beat Strytor!" Tom looked up at the sound of Elenna's voice, and saw her rushing towards him, grinning.

Tom shook his head. "This isn't over yet."

Digging deep, he drew on the power of the golden helmet one last time. He gazed into the distance with magical vision, and saw a familiar hunched, cloaked figure shambling away over the edge of the plateau.

Jezrin!

The ice-cold tingle of infection surged through Tom's hand again, but he rose to his feet in spite of it.

"Don't you ever stop?" groaned Petra.

"No time for that," said Tom. "Jezrin has almost reached the Well of Power!"

5

JEZRIN'S FINAL TRICK

Tom stumbled across the plateau as fast as he could, scattering bones with every step and doing his best not to think about the throbbing pain in his hand. Elenna and Petra ran at his side, and Tom felt stronger and more confident knowing his friends were with him.

Together we can stop Jezrin! If we can only catch him...

They reached the edge of the plateau and ran down a short scree slope. Beyond it lay a valley filled with some of the biggest rocks Tom had seen yet. Massive boulders were piled on top of each other, forming towers that loomed over them like hulking ogres.

"Where is he?" asked Elenna anxiously.

Tom shook his head. "There's no way I could see him in there, even with the golden helmet. We'll have to go carefully."

He led the way, creeping in among the boulders, alert for any sound.

Jezrin might be lying in wait for us...

"There!" Petra gasped, suddenly.

Tom followed her pointing finger and saw a clearing up ahead, surrounded on all sides by rocky columns. Kneeling in the centre was the cloaked figure of the Evil Wizard.

The breath caught in Tom's throat as he saw three objects laid out in the dust in front of Jezrin. A purple horn, a glittering scale and a curved fang of ice. *The magical tokens!* Jezrin was muttering strange words in a low, deep voice, his hands held out with palms facing up.

"He's going to raise the well," said Petra, her own voice growing tight with horror.

"Not if I can help it," muttered Tom. He charged at the wizard, sword raised, but when he was just a few paces away, Jezrin flicked his left hand.

Fzzzapp! Tom struck a wall of light, face first. Magic jolted through

his body and threw him back. He
stumbled and collapsed on the
ground, his whole body buzzing with
pain.

"Tom!" cried Elenna.

Stars swam in Tom's vision as
he propped himself dizzily on one

elbow. A shimmering dome of energy had sprung up all around the Evil Wizard, glowing sickly yellow.

Behind his wall of magic, Jezrin turned to smirk at them. "And so the great hero arrives to save us all!" he sneered. "What a pity he has failed so completely. How does it feel, Master of the Beasts? To see that I have been one step ahead of you all this while? I knew the noble Tom could never resist this Quest. I knew you would battle the dragons and take their tokens. All I had to do was wait, then have my servant Rourke collect them for me. To think that foolish witch thought the crow was hers! It has all been so easy I am almost...disappointed!"

Tom lurched to his feet and struck the dome with his scaly fist. His hand was so numb with poison that he could hardly feel the magic jolting back into it. Even so, he couldn't break through the force-field.

Jezrin threw back his head and laughed. "How pathetic! Now all that's left is for the three of you to witness my triumph." His eyes glinted with greed. "Once I have drunk from the Well of Power, no one will dare stand in my way!"

Turning back to the three magical tokens that lay on the ground before him, Jezrin began muttering again.

Slowly at first, the ground began to shudder. Smaller rocks fell from the columns around them. A roar of thunder sounded in the distance, and the sky grew even darker, as though night was falling.

Elenna sent an arrow whizzing towards Jezrin, but as it struck his magical dome, the missile exploded into a shower of cinders.

Tom watched, frozen with horror, as the ground split in front of the Evil Wizard with a deafening crack. From the darkness below, a pedestal of red stone rose up, rumbling slowly into place. Its sides were intricately carved with images of flying dragons, and on top of it sat a red

stone basin of crystal-clear water.

"Can't you do something?" Elenna
shouted at Petra. "Cast a spell!"

The witch scowled. "You don't think I already thought of that? I can't break the force-field. Jezrin's magic is far too powerful!"

Tom desperately attacked the dome again, slamming it with his fist. *Hopeless*. He tried charging with his shield, throwing all his weight behind it, but the dome didn't even shudder at the impact. "This isn't over, Jezrin!" he shouted, over another rumble of thunder.

"Oh, I think it is," said Jezrin. The wizard rose, cupped his hands and scooped water from the basin into his mouth. The sky shook with an even louder thunderclap, and Jezrin laughed with savage joy.

Tom fell to his knees. *Jezrin's right. No one can stop him now.*

"Let me tell you, friends," said the wizard, "nothing in all the world tastes so sweet as power! And now I have every last drop for my…"

He trailed off as the magical dome began to flicker around him.

Tom blinked, hardly daring to trust his eyes. But it was really happening. The yellow light faded, then disappeared entirely.

Jezrin's brow furrowed with rage and confusion. He whirled round and glared at Petra. "You! What did you do, witch?" But Petra looked just as puzzled as Tom felt.

Jezrin flung out his hands as

though to cast a spell, but nothing happened. "What is this?" he shrieked. "That treacherous well stole my magic from me! But I did everything that was needed! I brought the magical tokens! I am—"

Unworthy! The voice sounded in Tom's mind. *You are unworthy of sssuch power, Jezzzzzrin... And you mussst pay the pricccccce!*

Tom knew that voice. Jezrin's eyes widened in horror at something he had seen in the darkened sky. A cold weight settled in Tom's stomach, as he turned to look for himself.

A terrifying creature loomed overhead. It soared closer, his bones glowing white. *Strytor!* The skeleton dragon was complete again, his wings beating the air, his mighty jaws clacking together like the slamming of a coffin lid.

"Take cover!" yelled Petra, diving behind a rock as Strytor swooped towards them. Tom spotted the red glimmer again, deep in the Beast's ribcage. It swirled and grew into a raging ball of fire, roared up into a jet of flame, then spewed from the dragon's bony mouth...

Jezrin stood rooted to the spot, his hands dripping with water. As the fire surged towards him, his robe billowed in the gust of Strytor's breath. "No!" screeched Jezrin. Then he was engulfed in a white-hot inferno, so bright that Tom had to look away.

When he turned back, Tom saw that the skeleton dragon had flown on overhead, and Jezrin was gone. A pile of ashes lay where the Evil

Wizard had been standing, and a few
cinders danced in the breeze. Tom
swallowed hard, fighting down the
shock.

"The stories say Strytor is
impossible to defeat," murmured
Petra, emerging from her hiding

place. "The magic of Drakonia will bring him back to life, over and over."

"Look out!" shouted Elenna. "He's coming back..."

Tom whirled round. Sure enough, he saw the skeleton dragon wheel in the sky and curve towards them. And when Strytor's voice sounded again in Tom's head, there was no trace of mercy in it.

You three, who ssseek to sssteal the watersss of the well! You mussst alssso pay...

THE BATTLE AT THE WELL

Another burst of flame streaked from Strytor's gaping mouth.

WHHHSSHHHH!

Tom rolled behind a boulder. He could feel the searing heat of the blast behind him, and hear the roar and crackle as it scorched the ground all around.

Peering round the side of the rock, he saw a large patch of blackened earth where the flames had struck. *But where's Elenna? Where's Petra?* His heart seemed to drop out of his chest, until he spotted his friends both huddling together in the shadow of one of the rocky columns.

Tom flung his shield up over his head. The magical dragon scale of Ferno, embedded in the shield, would protect him against the flames. Then he ran, crouching as low as he could, heading for a tall column closer to his companions.

Once again he heard a deafening *WHHHSSHHH*, and the column was engulfed by flames. The sheer force

of Strytor's breath sent it toppling,
shaking the ground as it fell. Tom
switched direction, darting left and
ducking down behind another pile
of rocks.

His poisoned hand was aching worse than ever, and his breath came fast and heavy. Chancing a quick glance upwards, he saw the skeleton dragon circling, his long neck snaking as he peered down, trying to spot his prey...

Tom threw himself flat, his mind racing. *If I could just get to Elenna and Petra, maybe we could defeat Strytor together! There has to be some way to bring the Beast down.*

But he couldn't think how.

Flinging up his shield again, Tom broke cover and ran, racing as fast as he could towards the column where his friends were sheltering.

WHHHSSHHHHHH!

The hiss of Strytor's breath sounded terrifyingly close this time, and suddenly Tom felt his heel burning with pain. He glanced over his shoulder, and saw flames licking up from his boot. *I'm on fire!* He hopped, desperately beating at the flames with his sword-hand until they smouldered out. But his other foot hit a rock and he sprawled headlong, elbows scraping on the hard ground.

Groaning with pain, Tom rolled over and saw Strytor drop out of the sky, both wings spread wide. Another ball of red fire was taking shape in the Beast's chest. Tom scrambled to his feet, but he knew there was no way he would reach cover in time. Any moment now, he would be burned to cinders...

"Don't move!" It was Petra's voice.

Tom whirled round to see the witch had rushed out from behind her column. She dived towards Tom, her hands twitching. *She's casting a spell!*

The next moment a blue light surged from Petra's fingertips, blindingly bright. Tom shut his eyes, and a sudden wave of freezing cold washed over him.

When he looked again, he found the witch standing beside him, panting with the effort of her magic. All around them a glittering blue

dome had appeared out of thin air, just like the one Jezrin had conjured up. *Except this dome is made of ice!*

Strytor's flame rained down from above, engulfing the dome, but the ice held firm. Tom shivered from the cold, and the thought of what would have happened without Petra's magic protecting them. "Thank you, Petra," he said.

The witch seemed too embarrassed to meet his eyes. "It was nothing," she mumbled. "It's not going to hold for long."

Looking up, Tom saw that she was right. The outer surface of the dome was already slippery with water, where the heat from Strytor's breath had melted the ice.

I will burn you, Avantiansss... hissed the voice of the Beast.

Through the curtain of water, Tom saw a blur of movement as Elenna stepped out of cover and sent an arrow streaking upwards at the skeleton dragon.

Strytor jerked away, and Tom realised that the arrow must have bounced off the Beast's breastbone. *Nice work, Elenna!*

The skeleton dragon let out a savage cry, then banked and made off with heavy wingbeats. As he raced towards the horizon, Strytor howled a second time – a long, rattling call so eerie it made the hairs on the back of Tom's neck rise.

It sounds almost as though the skeleton dragon is calling for help...

"How do we get out of here?" Tom asked, pointing at the icy dome.

Petra shrugged. "I saved your life – what more do you want?"

Tom grinned and kicked at the side of the melting dome. A big chunk of ice fell free. He hacked at the hole with his sword, making it bigger until he and Petra were able to scramble free. Shivering with cold, Tom rushed over to Elenna.

His friend was looking puzzled. "Why do you think Strytor flew away?" she asked.

"I think I have an idea why," said Petra, her voice trembling. She pointed, and Tom followed her gaze to the slopes of the bone plateau.

No! It can't be...

All across the plain, he could see white figures stirring – creatures made of bone, clambering to their feet. Some looked like humans, while others were lizard-people, wolves and even bears. As they rose, they began to run, charging down the scree slope at the edge of the plateau towards the rocky columns where Tom and his friends were standing.

Strytor was calling for help, Tom realised. *From an army of skeletons!*

1

FIGHT TO THE END

Strytor glided above the surging horde. His bone wings curved like sails, throwing his skeleton army into shadow.

"I'll handle the Beast," said Tom. "You hold off the bone creatures. Agreed?"

"Agreed," said Elenna, grimacing

as she glanced up at the gigantic skeleton dragon, looming closer and closer. "What do you say, Petra?"

The witch shrugged. "They're already dead. How hard can it be?"

The two of them stepped out to meet the skeletons that were clattering down the slope towards them. Elenna drew an arrow and fitted it to her bowstring, while Petra began muttering, preparing a spell.

Tom's heart surged at the determination of his friends. But he noticed that Elenna was running out of arrows, and that Petra looked pale and unsteady on her feet, after the effort of conjuring the dome of ice.

He turned his gaze on Strytor. Another fireball was already forming in his vast ribcage. *If the Beast keeps breathing fire at us, we really are finished! I need to get close enough to put out the flames...*

He darted forward, running past his friends as fast as he could. "Over here!" he shouted at Strytor. "Unless you're too scared to fight me one on one!"

Ssstrytor is ssscared of nothing! hissed the Beast's voice in his head.

Tom stopped dead and flung his arms out, exposing his chest. "Come on, then!"

"What are you doing, you fool?" yelled Petra.

But Tom didn't have time to reply. The skeleton dragon arched his wings and plummeted, landing on all four clawed feet in front of Tom with a sickening crunch that made the rocky columns tremble.

Tom sheathed his sword and let his shield hang by his side. The Beast stalked forward, his neck swaying like a snake about to strike.

Every muscle in Tom's body tensed to run, but he forced himself to stay

still. *Just a little closer....*

Then the fireball in Strytor's ribcage rushed up the dragon's neck, and a burning torrent of flame gushed towards Tom.

This time, he was ready for it. He threw himself into a forward roll, the flames licking at his heels, just where he'd been standing a moment before. He staggered upright within touching distance of the Beast's ribcage. The heat of it pulsed through his body, and sweat broke out on his brow. *Now I just need to get even closer!*

Tom raised his shield. He reached out with his good hand and grabbed hold of the nearest rib. It was searingly hot, and he almost let go at once. *No! Have to hold on...*

Heaving himself in through a gap between the ribs, Tom braced his boots against the bone. He clung on desperately with his good hand. The heat was almost unbearable, even behind his shield. But he didn't have a choice.

The ribs shook like an earthquake as Strytor let out a furious bellow. Tom's stomach lurched as he felt the Beast launch into the air. They rose fast, jerking upwards with Strytor's powerful wingbeats.

They were still climbing higher as Tom peered over the edge of his shield. The fireball hovering in the

middle of the ribcage had started
to writhe and swell once again.
The skeleton dragon's savage voice
hissed inside his head. *I will ssslay*

*you, Massster of the Beastsss, after I
have killed your friendsss!*

Craning his neck, Tom saw with
horror that Strytor was descending
again, speeding like a falcon
towards Elenna and Petra... His
friends were too busy battling the
skeleton army, firing arrows and
magical bolts of light, to see the
Beast bearing down on them.

Tom leant closer to the churning
fireball. The heat washed over his
shield, and sweat stung his eyes.
Closer... Closer... He shifted the
shield until it almost touched the
flames, blocking the pathway up the
dragon's neck.

His heart was pumping. *If this*

doesn't work, Elenna and Petra are going to die.

Strytor folded his wings, diving faster and faster. Tom threw another quick glance below and saw his friends look up. Their faces froze in fear. The Beast stretched out his neck, opened his jaw...and suddenly the ball of fire surged into life.

Tom closed his eyes and channelled all his strength into holding the shield steady. The fire struck it with a *WHOOMPH*, and his arm jerked back, his legs almost buckling. But he pushed harder, holding it firm as Ferno's dragon scale repelled the deadly heat. With nowhere else to go, the fire surged

back on itself, and the skeleton
dragon's ribcage filled with a
sweltering heat.

Strytor howled in pain, a pitiful
shriek, as his ribs were scorched

black by his own flames. The bones began to char and crack. Smoke billowed through the ribcage, stinging Tom's eyes and making him splutter, but the shield token held firm. *It's like being inside a gigantic oven!* He blinked away tears and saw one of the blackened ribs collapse in a shower of ash.

Suddenly Strytor's skull jerked in agony, and the Beast went limp. The flames died all at once, leaving only bitter smoke and ash.

Have I destroyed the skeleton dragon for good?

They began to plummet towards the ground. Trapped inside the smoke-filled body of Strytor, Tom caught a glimpse of Elenna and Petra backing away, as the horde of bone creatures surged closer and closer. He heard the whistle of the wind through Strytor's bones, as the Beast dropped with him inside.

When we land, Strytor's body is going to crush me to pieces! I have to get out from underneath...

Tom snatched hold of the blackened stub of one of Strytor's ribs and hauled himself out through the gap. With the last of his strength, and the ground rushing up fast, he leapt clear of the plunging skeleton dragon.

Quickly he drew on the power of his enchanted eagle feather to

slow his fall. *Too late!* He hit rock, hard, rolling over and over. Behind him, the earth shook with a bone-shattering *CRUNCH* as Strytor finally struck the ground.

Then something hard smashed into Tom's head, and the whole world went black.

THE MASTER'S REWARD

"Is he alive?"

The voice seemed to come from a very long way away. Tom groaned. Someone was shaking him, sending stabs of pain through his bruised body.

Everything hurts...

"He's moving!" said another voice.

Elenna!

"Tom, can you stand up?"

He tried to, but leaning on his bad hand sent a wave of pain and nausea through him. He slumped back down again.

"We need magic," said Elenna. "Petra, can't you heal him?"

"If I could, I would have done it already," retorted Petra. "It's no good, he's hurt too badly."

Tom's eyelids fluttered open for a moment, and he saw his friends standing over him. Beyond them, fallen bone creatures lay jumbled on the ground. *They must have collapsed at the same time as Strytor.*

"I've got an idea," said Elenna.

Tom felt his friend hook her hands under his arms and begin to heave him across the rocks. He gritted his teeth to stop himself from crying out. He could hardly tell what hurt most – the pulsing infection in his hand and arm, the thundering in his head, the throbbing of his limbs...

"Give me a hand," grunted Elenna, and Tom felt Petra take hold of his ankles. His friends lifted him up off the rocks, carrying him along.

Tom didn't know where they were going. It was all he could do to stay conscious. *Got to...hold on...* He had a horrible feeling that if he let himself fall asleep, he might never wake up again.

He felt himself being lifted upright.

"Here," said Elenna, finally.

Opening his eyes, Tom saw that they had draped him over the red stone podium of the Well of Power. He gripped on to the stone with weakened fingers, his head hanging over the water. He could see his own face reflected in its crystal-clear surface, as pale as a corpse's.

"Drink," said Elenna.

Tom shook his head.

"Don't be an idiot," snapped Petra. "It's your only hope!"

But Tom couldn't shake the image of Jezrin drinking from the well and

losing all his magic. *What if the well takes my powers too? I'd rather die than lose them.* Perhaps he was no worthier than Jezrin.

You are worthy, Massster of the Beassstss!

Tom looked up as the voice sounded in his head. A short distance away, Strytor the Skeleton Dragon was clambering to his feet once more, his body clattering ominously. Tom watched as the Beast's blackened bones clicked into place, turning yellow-white again.

"I don't understand," said Elenna. "You've destroyed that dragon twice now!"

"I told you, it's the magic of Drakonia," said Petra. "Don't worry, Tom, we'll hold off the Beast. Just stay still and—"

"No," Tom grunted. "Don't... attack." Somehow he felt sure that the Beast wasn't going to fight them.

Strytor's voice echoed in his head again. *You risssked your life to sssave your friendsss... You are worthy to drink from the Well of Power.*

The Beast's head hovered lower on his massive, winding neck. His jaw opened, and a fresh flame kindled in his newly formed ribcage. But this time Tom felt no fear. He watched silently as a thin tongue of flame travelled up Strytor's neck and streamed from his mouth, straight into the well.

The water bubbled and spurted, and steam rose from it with a soft hiss. Tom breathed in deeply, his nostrils filling with a sweet, flowery scent. He dipped his poisoned hand into the well, and the water felt cool against his skin.

A silver shimmer spread through the basin, and Tom peered closer, hardly daring to believe what he was seeing. The brown scales on his wrist were fading away. *The water is healing me!* He moved his fingers in astonishment, and it gave him no pain at all.

A moment later the scales had disappeared entirely, and Tom's hand felt as good as new. He looked up into the gaping dark of Strytor's empty eye sockets, and at last he understood. *There were four tokens all along. The horn, the scale, the*

ice fang...and Strytor's flame! No
wonder the well's magic didn't work
for Jezrin.

Tom leaned over the basin and
scooped water into his mouth. It

tasted sweet and cold, and with each gulp he could feel the aches and pains of the fight drain out of him. When he lifted his head and wiped his mouth, he knew he was back to his old self at last. *Maybe even better than before!*

Drawing on the power of his red jewel, Tom spoke to the skeleton dragon. *Thank you, Strytor.*

The Beast nodded slowly, and his voice hissed in reply. *Worthy heroesss will alwaysss be welcome in Drakonia!* Then Strytor reared up on his hind legs, spread his wings and rose into the sky with ragged flaps.

Tom watched the skeleton dragon

disappear into a sky which had turned bright blue once again, until the Beast was nothing but a distant white speck above the mountains.

"You look better, Tom," said Elenna.

Tom turned to his smiling friends and grinned back at them. "I feel better too," he said. "Especially now that Jezrin is finally gone for good. I think it might be time to leave Drakonia to the Drakonians."

"Back to Avantia, then," said Petra. Her face fell. "Perhaps I'll find a new pet raven there."

"Of course you will," said Elenna, laying a hand on the witch's shoulder. "If we can get home, that is... We'll need a dragon to leave this place."

"Oh, I'll take care of that," said Petra. "Watch this." The witch closed her eyes and began muttering the words of a spell.

"Look!" gasped Elenna, a moment later.

Tom gazed at the horizon. Strytor had finally disappeared, but two more specks were growing larger and larger, swooping through the sky towards them. One shape was green, the other red.

Tom gaped. "It's Vedra and Krimon!"

"Petra, did you summon them from Rion?" said Elenna.

"Not just them," said the witch, opening her eyes and looking smug.

More dots were appearing in the sky – dragons of all shapes and sizes, flapping towards them in a great swarm, so many that they filled the sky, their scales flashing every colour of the rainbow.

As they circled and swooped among the clouds, Tom couldn't help laughing. There were so many dragons in the sky – he didn't even know all of their names. It seemed as though Petra had called every Good dragon in all the known kingdoms.

Elenna clapped him on the shoulder. "Well, Master of the

Beasts," she said. "What are we waiting for?"

Tom grinned at her. "Another Quest complete," he said. "Now...let's go home!"

THE END

CONGRATULATIONS, YOU HAVE COMPLETED THIS QUEST!

At the end of each chapter you were awarded a special gold coin. The QUEST in this book was worth an amazing 8 coins.

Look at the Beast Quest totem picture inside the back cover of this book to see how far you've come in your journey to become

MASTER OF THE BEASTS.

The more books you read, the more coins you will collect!

Do you want your own
Beast Quest Totem?

1. Cut out and collect the coin below
2. Go to the Beast Quest website
3. Download and print out your totem
4. Add your coin to the totem

www.beastquest.co.uk/totem

Don't miss the first exciting Beast Quest book in this series, QUARG THE STONE DRAGON!

Read on for a sneak peek...

A TERRIBLE HOMECOMING

Tom's body swayed gently in time with Storm's hoofbeats. In the saddle behind him, Elenna let out a contented yawn. Feathery streaks of pink and gold painted the evening sky. The fierce heat of the day had

ebbed as they rode. A welcome
breeze, sweet with the smell of sun-
baked grass, cooled the sweat on
Tom's face.

Avantia had been so calm since
Tom and Elenna completed their
latest Quest that King Hugo had
granted them leave to visit Tom's
home village, Errinel. Excitement
swelled in Tom's chest at the thought
of seeing his aunt and uncle again.
He spotted a swift shadow loping
towards them across the fields. A
moment later Silver, Elenna's wolf,
took his place at Storm's side.

"Hello, boy!" Elenna said. "Did you
catch anything good?"

Silver looked up at her, his eyes

bright points in the gloom. He licked his muzzle.

"I'll take that as a yes," Elenna said. "I could do with some supper too! It's getting late. Do you think we should set up camp?"

Tom shook his head. "If we press on, we should reach Errinel before Aunt Maria and Uncle Henry turn in – maybe even in time for dinner."

"Sounds good to me," Elenna said. "I'd much prefer to sleep in a bed tonight than on the ground."

They followed the road onwards, past darkening fields and dusky copses of trees echoing with the melodies of hidden birds. Gradually, everything fell silent about them except for the steady clop of Storm's hooves. Stars blinked into life one by one until the wide, moonless sky glittered with their light.

Tom flexed his tired shoulders as Storm rounded the last bend of their journey. The lights of his village came into view, along with the comforting sight of chimney smoke curling into the sky. But as they neared Errinel, Tom felt his horse's steps falter and slow. Storm's head went up and his ears flicked back. Tom squeezed Storm's flanks with his knees.

"Keep going, boy," he said. "There are oats and a cosy stable ahead!"

Behind them, Silver let out an

uneasy growl. Tom glanced back to see the wolf's hackles raised and his sharp teeth bared.

"What's up, Silver?" Elenna asked.

Tom couldn't see anything ahead except the silhouettes of houses, broken by the soft glow of doors and windows left open to let in the warm night air.

"We'd best be on our guard," Elenna said.

Tom nodded and loosened his sword in its sheath. As Storm passed between the first cottages, the sound of the stallion's hoof beats echoed strangely. Tom's skin prickled.

"It's too quiet," he said.

He pulled Storm to a halt and

dropped from the saddle with Elenna at his side. They signalled for the animals to wait and crossed to the nearest cottage. As they entered, Tom heard the rustle of last embers of a dying fire settling in the grate. The guttering light from a candle stub cast bobbing shadows across the walls.

"Hello?" Tom called. But his voice fell dead in the empty silence. He and Elenna exchanged puzzled frowns.

"Let's try the next house," Elenna said.

There, plates of food lay half eaten on the table. The dining chairs had been pushed back crookedly, and

a pitcher of water lay on its side,
spilling a dark puddle on to the floor.

"Where is everyone?" Elenna asked.

Tom's pulse quickened. "Let's try

the forge," he said. As they stepped back into the night, the tang of sweet, acrid smoke caught in Tom's throat. He frowned. *Burning sugar?*

The smell grew stronger as he and Elenna followed the deserted street. Soon Tom could see smoke billowing from the open door of his uncle's cottage. His heart gave a skip of fear.

I hope Henry and Maria are all right.

He and Elenna rushed inside to find smoke streaming from around the edge of the stove door. Tom threw it open. More smoke billowed out, stinging his eyes. When it cleared, Tom saw a blackened pie.

What's going on here?

"Everyone can't have just vanished!" he said.

Elenna glanced about the cottage, frowning. "Nothing's been damaged," she said. "And I don't see any sign of a Beast attack or any dark magic. The fact that no one's here might be a good sign. Whatever happened, everyone escaped."

Tom took in the familiar details of his aunt's tidy kitchen and the table set with butter and jam. *Elenna's right*, he told himself. But still, he couldn't shake the worry gnawing inside him.

"Let's check the town hall," he said. "Maybe everyone's there."

He and Elenna left the forge

behind, passing more empty houses and deserted side streets, until they reached the main square. Apart from the quiet bubbling of the town's stone fountain, silence greeted them. The windows of the town hall shone darkly in the flickering torchlight that lit the square…

And in its shadow, a dark silhouette was crouched.

Read
QUARG THE STONE DRAGON
to find out what happens next!

Fight the Beasts,
Fear the Magic

Do you want to know more
about BEAST QUEST?
Then join our Quest Club!

Visit
www.beastquest.co.uk/club
and sign up today!

Are you a collector of the Beast Quest Cards?
Visit the website for further information.